Kevin and Katie written and illustrated by Liesbet Slegers
Original title: Karel en Kaatje
Translated from Dutch by Inge Van den Abeele-Kinget
Edited by Hannele Rubin

ISBN 978-1-60537-014-9

Manufactured in China
First Edition
10 9 8 7 6 5 4 3 2 1

Kevin and Katie

Liesbet Slegers

Clavis
NEW YORK

Hi, I am Kevin.

Next to my house there is another house.

A new family moved in.

They are our new neighbors.

My new neighbor is Katie.
Today she will visit me.
We will play together.
It will be fun!

Katie's mom and my mom
are sitting on the porch.
They talk and talk.
They are already friends.

"Come on, Katie, let's play.
This is my new train.
Choo choo. Choo choo.
Don't you want to play?"

"I am on my rocking horse.
You can ride my cart.
Watch out, Knight Kevin is coming!
Wheeee! We are going fast!"

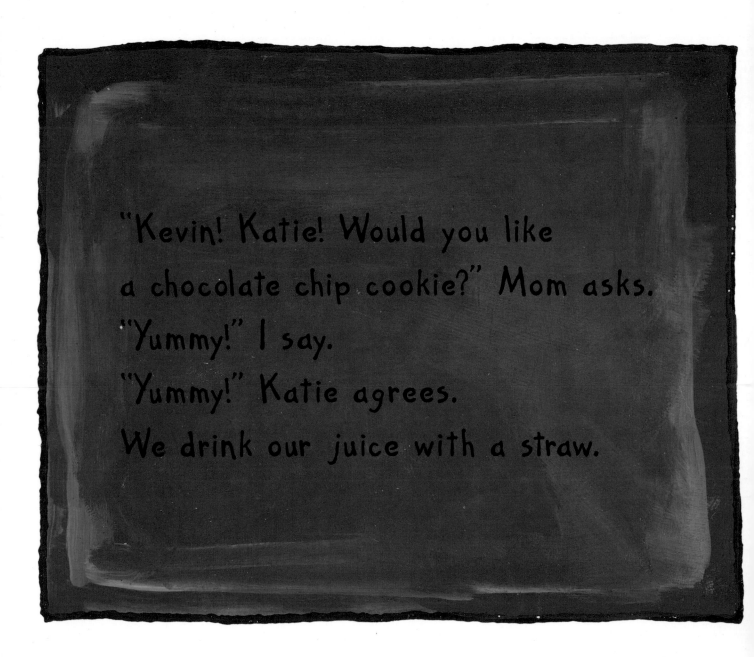

"Kevin! Katie! Would you like
a chocolate chip cookie?" Mom asks.
"Yummy!" I say.
"Yummy!" Katie agrees.
We drink our juice with a straw.

"Look, Katie, this is my teddy bear."
"This is my bunny," Katie says.
"I think Teddy and Bunny want to play together," Katie says.
Katie takes my teddy bear.

"No! Teddy is mine!" I cry.
"Katie, give Kevin back his bear,"
Katie's mom says.
"You can't take things away from others."

Katie gives me my teddy bear back.
She also gives me her bunny.
"Here, you can play with my bunny,"
she says. I'm smiling again.

"That's nice," I say.
"Let's put Bunny and Teddy in the stroller.
Now they are friends, just like us!"

"Let's pretend we have a store.
What would you like to buy, Miss?
Apples or bananas?" I ask.
"Two apples, please!" Katie says.
"One for Bunny and one for Teddy."

It's getting late.

Katie has to go home with her mom.

"Bye, Kevin. See you tomorrow.

Maybe you can play at my house,"

Katie says.